Everybody Bakes Bread

by Norah Dooley
illustrations by Peter J. Thornton

Carolrhoda Books, Inc. / Minneapolis

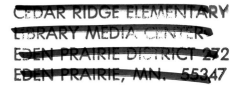

A special thank you to my neighbors for their friendship and recipes:
Mrs. Edlin Ambrose; Ms. Crystal Bourne; Oscar, Mayra, Bernardo,
and Becky Chacon; Mrs. Agnes Darlington; Gail Leicher; Mrs. Geneva
Licorish; Ann-Marie, Shirley, and Mark-Anthony Licorish; Debbie
Max; Blanca Polio; Nabil and Amalia Sater; and the Middle East
Restaurant, Cambridge, Massachusetts. Thanks to my mother,
Adelaide Dooley, for her recipes, love, and support; my husband,
Robert Fairchild, for his love and support; and our four inspirational
critics, Sira, Julia, Ferron, and Rosalie.   —N.D.

Thank you to Ben, Ruth, Alison, Ana, Punleu, Vikki, Mary Louise,
Hira, Daniel, Wendy, Chantal, Marie, Frank, Micah, Nick, Bunny,
Alicia, Michael, and especially Lily.   —P.J.T.

This book is available in two editions:
Library binding by Carolrhoda Books, Inc.
Soft cover by First Avenue Editions
c/o The Lerner Group
241 First Avenue North, Minneapolis, MN 55401

Library of Congress Cataloging-in-Publication Data

Dooley, Norah.
   Everybody bakes bread / by Norah Dooley ; illustrations by Peter J.
Thornton.
       p. cm.
   Summary: A rainy-day errand introduces Carrie to many different
kinds of bread, including chapatis, challah, and pupusas. Includes
recipes.
   ISBN 0-87614-864-X (lib. bdg.)—ISBN 0-87614-895-X (pbk.)
   [1. Bread—Fiction. 2. Baking—Fiction.] I. Thornton, Peter J., ill.
II. Title.
PZ7.D7265Ev   1996
[E]—dc20   95-6054
                                                    CIP
                                                     AC

Manufactured in the United States of America
1 2 3 4 5 6 - SP - 01 00 99 98 97 96

To all who "feed the hungry"
                    —N.D.

For Mom and Dad
                    —P.J.T.

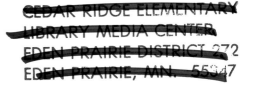

It was another rainy Saturday. Why did it always have to rain on the weekend? At least it could snow instead. We were supposed to play kickball today, but nobody would come out in all this rain.

Mom was making my great-grandmother's Italian bread with me and Anthony. He's my little brother, and he was really getting on my nerves.

"Carrie, that is enough!" Mom had that dangerous sound in her voice.

"But I never get a turn at kneading," I said. I kneaded Anthony's arm to make him move. He squawked and the bread dough fell on the floor.

"Quiet, you two!" scolded Mom. "Anna is sleeping."

We made faces at each other while Mom sighed and stared out the window at the rain. She turned around and raised one eyebrow. "Carrie, why don't you go ask Mrs. Ambrose and Crystal if they have a three-handled rolling pin we can use?"

"Okay," I said. I like to run errands.

"I want to go, too!" whined Anthony.

"Then you'll miss the braiding and the baking," Mom reminded him. Anthony thought about it, then smiled and stuck out his tongue at me.

"Is the rolling pin for baking, Mom?" I asked, pulling on my boots and raincoat.

"Just tell them what we're doing and that I need one," she said with a funny little smile.

"Can I ask around the neighborhood?"

"Just be back for lunch," said Mom.

There were only a few interesting puddles on the way to Mrs. Ambrose's house, so I got there pretty quickly. It took them a while to answer their door, since Mrs. Ambrose uses a cane and her cousin Crystal has a bad hip. But I didn't mind, because their entry smelled like fresh coconut bread. And next to Barbadian fish cakes, I think I like Barbadian coconut bread best. Crystal let me in, and I told her why I was there. She laughed quietly as I climbed the stairs slowly behind her.

Upstairs, Mrs. Ambrose said, "Sit down a moment, girl. Test some of this bread come fresh out the oven."

I was right. There, on a cooling rack, were two big loaves of coconut bread. Mrs. Ambrose cut me an end piece and a puff of steam came out. The bread was heavy in my hand. It was packed with raisins and sweet with coconut. "What should I tell my mom about the rolling pin?" I asked between bites.

"Ohhh, tell her we loaned it to our niece," said Mrs. Ambrose.

"But you're welcome to come back anytime your mother needs something," added Crystal sweetly.

"Thanks for the bread," I called as I clomped down the stairs.

It was raining harder than ever when I went to Rajit's house. His mom has lots of interesting things to cook with. Besides, Rajit is a good kickball player, and if enough kids would come out, maybe we could have a rainy kickball game. Rajit's mom answered the door.

"Carrie! Come in, come in! What brings you out in this weather?" she asked. After I explained about our bread making and my errand, she said, smiling, "Well, I will check for you. But I was just making chapatis—Indian bread—with Rajit and his brother. Perhaps you would like to help?"

We made the most delicious flat bread, right in a frying pan. It was very chewy and nutty tasting. Rajit and Sonjit agreed to play kickball after lunch if I could get some other kids. Their mom couldn't find the rolling pin, so I said good-bye and went to see Mark DeLoach.

I had to ring and ring before Mark heard the bell. He was listening to some loud music.

"What d'ya want?" he said when he finally answered the door. I explained the game plan on our way into the kitchen. His older sisters, Anne-Marie and Shirley, were washing dishes. Mark started to pick at a pan of fresh corn bread on the table, so I did, too. It tasted really buttery, and it was just plain old corn bread, with nothing on it. Mrs. DeLoach comes from South Carolina, and her corn bread is the best.

Anne-Marie turned around and saw us snacking. "Stop picking at that! It's for the church dinner," she hollered.

"That's all right." Their mom came into the kitchen. "This little one is just for the nibblin' rabbits 'round here," she said. Mrs. DeLoach opened the oven and showed us a much bigger pan of corn bread inside. "The big one's goin' to the church. But y'all, please eat like folks with manners," she said, handing us plates and a knife.

"Oh, I forgot to ask," I said. "Have you got a three-handled rolling pin my mom could borrow?"

"My old pin hasn't got but two handles," said Mrs. DeLoach, looking at me really funny, her nose wrinkling like she had to sneeze. "Y'all can ask her if she needs my three-legged ladle, though."

Anne-Marie and Shirley laughed. I did, too—even though I didn't really get the joke.

"I'll tell her," I said as I left. "And thanks for the corn bread."

Nabil and his sister, Amalia, live with their mom, dad, and grandma above the Middle East Oasis Restaurant and Bakery, which their dad runs. They have lots of different stuff in the restaurant kitchen, so I thought I'd check there.

Grandma Sater answered the apartment door. She is always nice to me and Anthony. Whenever she sees us pass by the restaurant, she gives us free pastries. She is from Lebanon and is very shy about speaking English, so Nabil and Amalia usually translate her Arabic for us. I asked for Nabil and Amalia with my best manners.

"Not here," said Mrs. Sater. "Come downstairs." She pointed at a door behind her. "Follow me."

We went into the restaurant kitchen, where everyone was busy getting ready for Saturday lunch. I looked around but didn't see any rolling pins. Nabil and Amalia were helping their uncle take balloon-shaped things out of an oven.

"Is this pocket bread?"
I asked.

"Yep," answered Nabil.

"I love the way it looks when it's puffy!" I said.

"Nabil and I call it 'cloth bread' when it's this fresh, 'cause it's so soft," said Amalia as we brought a basket of bread upstairs.

The bread flattened as it cooled, and it was just like a damp cloth. You could roll it or fold it or scrunch it into a ball.

I told Nabil and Amalia about the kickball plan while we ate fresh bread with a thick dip called hummus. They told me to ring their bell with our special code after lunch, and they would come right down.

On my way back from the Saters', I was swinging around parking meters and not really paying attention. That's how I forgot about the huge puddle where the storm sewer backs up.

"Look out!" warned a small voice behind me. Too late. A car went zooming by, and water splashed right over my head. I was soaked—even in my raincoat. It was Mrs. Max who had called out. She was wet, too.

"Come in with me, Carrie, and dry off a minute. Maybe have some tea?" she suggested.

I like Mrs. Max. Sometimes I help her with her grocery bags, and she gives me cups of tea in beautiful china she says came from the old country. Mrs. Max lives by herself, right in front of that puddle, in the old brick apartments.

Mrs. Max said she was all dressed up because today was the Jewish Sabbath, and she had gone to temple. While she changed, I got a basin of hot water to soak our feet. We sat with towels on our heads and cups of tea in our laps.

"I like this bread," I said.

"This is challah," said Mrs. Max. "I make a loaf every Friday."

"It's braided, like my mom's. But yours is very yellow and nice and sweet," I said.

"Yes. It has a lot of eggs in it. And some sugar. Would you like more tea?" asked Mrs. Max. "And you still haven't told me what you were doing out on a day like today."

"Well, we were baking bread today. Anthony and I were fighting, so my mom asked me to run an errand for her. Say, do you have a three-handled rolling pin?"

"A three-handled rolling pin? Your mother sent you for this?" Mrs. Max was quiet for a moment, but her eyes were twinkling. Finally she said, "How would you use that third handle, do you think?"

"Hmmm," I said, thinking this out. "Oh no," I groaned.

"Oh yes," Mrs. Max answered. "Your mother played a trick on you, perhaps?" I laughed out loud. So did Mrs. Max.

I felt warm again, and it was past noon. We still needed one more player for kickball, so I said thanks and left for my last stop before home.

Our new neighbors upstairs are from El Salvador, and their son Bernardo is about my age. He has been watching us kids from the second-floor window, so I thought he might be interested in the kickball game.

His little sister Becky looked out through the mail slot. She's just two years old and babbles nonstop in two languages—Spanish and English—all mixed together. She was telling me about our cat, I think. Bernardo's grandmother opened the door. She led me into the kitchen, where Bernardo was eating something round and yellow with melted cheese coming out of it.

"Hi," I said kind of shyly.

"Hi," he answered softly. Maybe he was shy, too.

"Eat?" asked his grandma as she set down a plate for me.

"Thank you. What is this?" I asked, taking a big bite.

"A pupusa," said Bernardo.

"You like it?" asked his grandma.

"Yes! Thank you," I replied, popping the last bite into my mouth. "Bernardo, can you play kickball with us after lunch?"

"Let me ask," he said.

Bernardo talked to his grandma, and looking out at the rain, she shrugged her shoulders but said, *"Sí."*

I said *gracias*—that's "thanks" in Spanish—and went down the back stairs to our house.

When I opened our back door, the kitchen smelled great.

"I got to do all the braiding myself," boasted Anthony.

"Did you have a good walk?" asked Mom, busy with Anna.

"Yes. No one had that rolling pin. But you can borrow Mrs. DeLoach's three-legged ladle anytime you want," I said, giving her my best one-eyebrow-up look.

Mom looked up and saw my face. "Oh. I guess you found me out."

"Yep," I said. "But I also found enough kids to play kickball, so can I play? If I wear boots and everything?

"Yes, you can play, but *after* you have lunch," said Mom.

"Lunch?" I said, finishing a piece of warm Italian bread dipped in olive oil and garlic. "I couldn't eat another bite. Practically everybody was baking bread this morning!"

Mrs. Ambrose's Coconut Bread

1½ cups butter or margarine, softened
3 tablespoons shortening
1¾ cups sugar
¾ cup milk
¾ cup water
1 teaspoon vanilla or almond extract
6 cups sifted flour
2 tablespoons baking powder
1½ teaspoons salt
1 teaspoon cinnamon
½ teaspoon nutmeg
3 cups shredded coconut
½ cup raisins (optional)

1. Preheat oven to 350°.
2. Grease 3 loaf pans.
3. In a large bowl, combine butter, shortening, and sugar. Beat with a spoon until light and fluffy.
4. Add milk, water, and flavoring and stir well.
5. Sift together flour, baking powder, salt, cinnamon, and nutmeg. Add flour mixture to butter mixture little by little, stirring after each addition.
6. Stir in coconut and raisins.
7. On a floured surface, shape dough into 3 loaves. Place loaves in pans.
8. Bake for 45 to 60 minutes or until a toothpick inserted in middle of bread comes out clean.

Makes 3 loaves

Rajit and Sonjit's Chapatis

2 cups whole wheat flour
2 tablespoons butter or margarine, chilled and
  cut into pea-sized pieces
1 teaspoon salt
1 cup warm water

1. Place flour and butter in a large bowl. Use your fingertips to rub butter into flour until mixture forms large crumbs.
2. In a small bowl, combine salt and water. Stir until salt has completely dissolved.
3. Add salt water to flour mixture little by little, mixing well with hands after each addition.
4. Knead dough in bowl for 10 minutes or until it is smooth and stretchy.
5. Cover bowl with damp cloth and let sit for 30 minutes.
6. Roll dough into walnut-sized balls. With a floured rolling pin, roll each ball into a 5-to 6-inch circle on a floured surface.
7. Heat a heavy frying pan over medium-high heat for about 5 minutes. (You can also use an electric frying pan.) Cook each chapati 1 to 2 minutes per side, until the edges curl and light brown spots begin to appear.

Makes 12 to 15 chapatis

Mrs. DeLoach's Corn Bread

1 cup yellow cornmeal
1 cup sifted all-purpose flour
2 teaspoons baking powder
1 teaspoon baking soda
1 teaspoon salt
2 tablespoons sugar
1 egg, beaten
1 cup milk
3 tablespoons melted butter or shortening

1. Preheat oven to 425°.
2. Grease a 9-by-9-inch pan.
3. Mix cornmeal, flour, baking powder, baking soda, salt, and sugar together in a large bowl.
4. Make a hollow in the middle of the cornmeal mixture. Add egg, milk, and melted butter and stir well.
5. Pour batter into pan. Bake for 20 to 25 minutes or until a toothpick stuck into the center comes out clean.

Makes 12 pieces

Nabil and Amalia's Pocket Bread

2 packages (2 tablespoons) active dry yeast
¼ teaspoon sugar
2 cups warm water (between 105° and 115°)
1 teaspoon salt
6 cups sifted all-purpose flour

1. In a large bowl, combine yeast, sugar, and ¼ cup warm water and stir. Let sit for 5 minutes. Stir in remaining water and salt.
2. Stir in flour little by little until dough begins to form a ball.
3. Place dough on a floured surface. Work in remaining flour with your hands. Then knead dough until it is smooth and stretchy.
4. Cover dough with a towel and let rise for about 45 minutes or until dough doubles in size.
5. Place a cookie sheet in the oven and preheat oven to 475°.
6. Punch down dough. Divide dough into 6 equal pieces. Cut each sixth into 4 pieces and roll each piece into a ball. You will make 24 balls. With a floured rolling pin, roll each ball into a 5- to 6-inch circle, ¼ inch thick.
7. Fill cookie sheet with dough circles, making sure they don't touch. Be careful not to burn yourself on the hot pan. Cover remaining dough with a damp towel. Bake on the bottom shelf of the oven for 4 to 5 minutes or until bread is golden brown and puffy. (They will flatten as they cool.)
8. Continue with remaining circles of dough. Be sure to heat pan up again after each batch.

Makes 24 pieces

Mrs. Max's Challah

1 package (1 tablespoon) active dry yeast
¼ cup sugar
1 cup warm water (between 105° and 115°)
6½ cups sifted all-purpose flour
1 tablespoon salt
3 eggs, slightly beaten
2 tablespoons vegetable oil

Egg wash:
1 egg yolk
2 tablespoons water

1. In a small bowl, combine yeast, 1 teaspoon of the sugar, and ¼ cup warm water and stir. Let sit for 5 minutes.
2. Place 5 cups of flour in a large bowl and make a deep hollow in the center. Pour yeast mixture into hollow.
3. Add remaining sugar, remaining water, salt, and 3 eggs and stir well.
4. Stir in additional flour little by little until a ball of dough forms.
5. Place dough on a floured surface. Work in remaining flour with your hands. Knead dough until it is smooth and stretchy.
6. Coat the inside of a large bowl with vegetable oil. Place the dough in the bowl and cover with a towel. Let rise in a warm place for about 45 minutes or until dough doubles in size.
7. Preheat oven to 350°.
8. Punch down dough. Divide dough into thirds. Cut each third in half. You will have 6 pieces of dough. On a floured board, roll each piece of dough into a 6-inch "rope."

9. Place 3 ropes of dough side by side. Braid dough, tucking the ends under. Repeat with remaining 3 strips.
10. In a small bowl, stir together egg yolk and water to make an egg wash.
11. Place loaves on a cookie sheet and brush lightly with egg wash.
12. Bake for 30 to 35 minutes until golden brown.

Makes 2 loaves

Bernardo's Pupusas

Masa harina is a corn flour that can be found in the gourmet section of a grocery store or in a grocery that specializes in Mexican and South American foods.

4 cups masa harina
1 teaspoon salt
2 cups hot water
¾ cup shredded cheese or refried beans
2 tablespoons vegetable oil

1. In a large bowl, combine salt and water and stir until salt is dissolved.
2. Add masa harina and stir.
3. Roll dough into 8 balls the size of golf balls. With your hands, pat each ball into a 3-inch circle, ¼ inch thick.
4. Make an indentation in the center of 4 of the circles with your fingers. Place about 2 teaspoons of shredded cheese or refried beans or a combination of both in each indentation. Place a second circle of dough on top of each circle and press the edges together.
5. Place oil in a large frying pan and heat over medium-high heat for about 5 minutes. Fry pupusas in pan for about 5 minutes per side or until golden brown. Drain on paper towel.

Makes 4 pupusas

Great-Grandmother's Italian Bread

¼ package (1 tablespoon) active dry yeast
1 teaspoon sugar
2 cups warm water (between 105° and 115°)
7 cups sifted all-purpose flour
1 teaspoon salt
2 teaspoons plus 2 tablespoons olive oil
¼ cup cornmeal

1. In a large bowl, combine yeast, sugar, and ¼ cup warm water and stir. Let sit for 5 minutes. Add remaining water.
2. Add 3 cups of flour and mix well (about 300 strokes). Stir in 2 teaspoons olive oil and salt.
3. Continue to stir in flour little by little until dough begins to form a ball.
4. Place dough on a floured surface. Knead in flour until dough is smooth and stretchy. (You may have some flour left over.)
5. Coat the inside of a large bowl with remaining olive oil. Place the dough in the bowl and cover with a towel. Let rise in a warm place for about 1 hour or until dough doubles in size.
6. Punch down dough and place on floured surface. Knead again for about 5 minutes.
7. Divide dough in half. Form each piece into a flat 10-by-10-inch loaf. Slice each loaf into 3 long strips.
8. Place 3 strips of dough side by side. Braid dough, tucking the ends under. Repeat with remaining 3 strips.
9. Sprinkle 2 cookie sheets with cornmeal. Place each loaf on a cookie sheet and cover with a towel. Let rise for 20 minutes.
10. Preheat oven to 400°.
11. Bake for 5 minutes. Reduce heat to 325° and bake for another 30 minutes. For a hard crust, spray loaves lightly with cold water every 5 minutes while baking.

Makes 2 loaves